COOL CAREERS WITHOUT COLLEGE ™

COOL CAREERS WITHOUT COLLEGE FOR PEOPLE WHO LOVE THE ARTS

TRACY BROWN HAMILTON

ROSEN PUBLISHING®
New York

Published in 2017 by The Rosen Publishing Group, Inc.
29 East 21st Street, New York, NY 10010

First Edition

Library of Congress Cataloging-in-Publication Data

Names: Hamilton, Tracy Brown, author.
Title: Cool careers without college for people who love the arts / Tracy Brown Hamilton.
Description: New York : Rosen Publishing, 2017. | Series: Cool careers without college | Includes bibliographical references and index.
Identifiers: LCCN 2016018109 | ISBN 9781508172888 (library bound)
Subjects: LCSH: Arts—Vocational guidance—Juvenile literature.
Classification: LCC NX163 .H36 2016 | DDC 700/.23—dc23
LC record available at https://lccn.loc.gov/2016018109

Manufactured in China

CONTENTS

INTRODUCTION

The world of the arts appeals to many people. Being part of a profession that has creativity at its core and getting the chance to contribute to making something that an audience appreciates is very satisfying. The energy, talent, and enthusiasm involved in careers in the arts make them exciting and ever changing.

Some people are drawn to performing. They enjoy sharing their gifts—as actors, dancers, comedians, or other artists—with appreciative audiences. Others are happier to work behind the scenes, building sets or making costumes for the theater, for example. Still others are passionate about writing songs or plays.

If you are someone who longs for a career in the arts but believe it is out of reach, don't be discouraged. It's true that many professions in the art world are highly competitive and that for many such jobs—actor, fine art painter, novelist, among others—a university degree or a master's

Whether the work happens behind a camera or behind the scenes, there are a number of careers in the arts that don't require a college degree.

of fine arts in a given subject is recommended. But there are other paths to achieving success and making your dream a reality.

A degree in the arts does not guarantee you a job. It provides you training and access to a network of other people with the same dream as you, but it is by no means the only way of gaining experience or honing your skills.

Key to your success in the arts is talent, ambition, and a refusal to give up. Artists in any field are constantly improving themselves and learning—from their peers, from their mentors, through self-study, or through workshops. The most important thing to do is to find a way to gain experience that showcases your talents and to have a personality and attitude that indicates you are committed and willing to learn and work hard.

People in the arts want to continue to grow, learn, and improve. They want to explore new areas and express new ideas. Art is never "done"—there is always more to do, more to create, and innovations that make artistic work dynamic.

The arts encompass many different areas: music, theater, film, dance, and other performing arts, as well as literature. And for each of these specific types of art, there are lots of people working behind the scenes. Writers have agents and editors who help them improve and sell their work. Actors have costume designers and makeup artists to help create the look they need for a role.

Engineers light a stage or ensure that the sound at a concert is the best it can be. Carpenters build sets for performing arts. There are business managers, lawyers, teachers, tailors, and merchandise manufacturers—all working in the arts.

This resource describes many traditional types of art-related careers and others that perhaps you have never considered. Most important, it tells you how you can pursue these professions while opting not to follow the college track. You'll find explanations of what each job entails, as well as tips for how best to prepare yourself to break into the field. You will also find information about the growth potential for each job.

Each section includes suggestions for other resources, as well as a profile of someone who does the job and how that person got started in his or her career.

CHAPTER 1

DANCER

Do you love to dance, to express feelings and convey stories through movement? Do you dream of performing for audiences on stage or on screen? If you have a gift for dance and are willing to dedicate yourself 100 percent to honing your skills, living and breathing dance, you might have what it takes to be a professional dancer.

The main job of a professional dancer is to entertain an audience. This includes:

- Studying many different forms of dance
- Keeping his or her body fit and healthy

Like athletes, professional dancers must spend a lot of time training and need to take good care of their bodies.

- Spending many hours a day practicing
- Auditioning for roles in a performance or in a dance company
- Attending promotional events to support performances in which he or she appears

Whether someone performs tap, ballet, modern dance, ballroom, or hip-hop, a career in dance is exciting, demanding, and competitive. Dancers can find work in theatrical performances or musicals. Others are hired to perform in music videos or commercials.

Unfortunately, only a small percentage of dancers ever find long-term, steady work. Most professional dancers belong to dance companies or troupes, while others are freelancers, scoring a job at a time while auditioning for the next. The work often requires frequent travel, for

Dancers have to compete with their peers in order to succeed in the field, so it's vital to have a strong sense of self-worth.

months at a time, to perform in locations around the world.

Men and women who make it as professional dancers often began serious training at a very young age. The career of a dancer is not as long as other, less physically demanding fields, so many dancers start young and retire relatively early. All successful dancers are continuously learning and perfecting their skills.

Dancing is hard on the body. According to the U.S. Bureau of Labor Statistics (http://www.bls.gov) professional dancers have one of the highest rates of on-the-job injuries. The physical demands are heavy: when dancers are not performing, they are often training or practicing up to eight hours a day. Dancers may also have to follow a strict diet.

Finding work as a dancer—particularly full-time, steady

A talented instructor can help many people learn to dance, including those who are interested only in dancing for their own enjoyment.

MADONNA'S BIG MOVE

Madonna is one of the most famous women in pop music and has also had success as an actress, director, and children's book author. Her first ambition, however, was to become a professional dancer. Madonna originally followed the college path, attending the dance program at the University of Michigan, where she'd earned a scholarship. She dropped out after two years, deciding that she was ready to get her artistic life started in the real world. She moved to New York City, where she began dancing with modern dance troupes while working as a waitress. She eventually became part of the Peter Lang Dance Theatre. Her move to New York was a daring one that paid off. In the Madonna biography *Madonna: Biography of the World's Greatest Pop Star,* Madonna is quoted as saying, "I came [to New York] with $35 in my pocket. It was the bravest thing I'd ever done."

work—is very difficult, so many dancers choose to join a union, such as the American Guild of Musical Artists. Being part of a union can help ensure a minimum salary, and members are informed of local auditions.

Succeeding as a dancer requires dedication and persistence. The work requires frequent auditioning, and because a large number of people are seeking work as a dancer, there is a lot of rejection involved. It's not enough to be good. You have to stand out from the crowd and be driven to succeed.

PREPARING YOURSELF

Training is a fundamental requirement for becoming a professional dancer. Many high schools have dance programs in which you can learn about the various types of dance, as well as emerging forms. If your high school does not have such a program, finding one given through a community center or local community college will give you the background and coaching you need to go from a good dancer to a pro.

Dancers must work to remain in good physical condition to do well in this field. Most successful dancers began taking dance lessons in their childhoods (some from as young as five years old), and dancers continue to train throughout their careers. You must be willing to make your dance training your top priority, which can mean spending most of your free time practicing. It takes a lot of dedication to make it as a dancer, as it is such a competitive field. Auditioning is also very important. Many dancers who choose not to follow a dance program at a college begin auditioning for full-time work as soon as they turn eighteen years old.

FUTURE PROSPECTS

Dancing is so physically demanding that it's not a career you can do forever. It's a good idea to have a plan for a second career relating to dance, such as teaching dance or becoming a choreographer. A choreographer is someone who designs and directs dance routines. Retired dancers often become dance directors, leading dancers who are performing in a play or other presentation. Keep in mind that because it is so difficult to find work as a dancer, many in the field have a second job such as teaching to bring in a steady income between dance jobs.

According to the Bureau of Labor Statistics, the job market for dancers and choreographers is expected to grow 5 percent from 2014 to 2024. According to the bureau's *Occupational Outlook Handbook*, "Growing interest in dance and in pop culture may provide opportunities in dance schools and in fields outside of dance companies."

FOR MORE INFORMATION

BOOKS

Butterworth, Jo. *Dance Studies: The Basics*. New York, NY: Routledge, 2012.

An introduction to the study of dance, this book covers choreography, technique, and the role of dance in different cultures.

Haas, Jacqui Greene. *Dance Anatomy*. Champaign, IL: Human Kinetics, 2010.

This book is a collection of more than two hundred illustrations showing the connection between muscle movement and creative expression.

Lefevre, Camille. *The Dance Bible: The Complete Resource for Aspiring Dancers*. New York, NY: Barron's Educational Series, 2012.

The Dance Bible is for all amateur dancers looking to turn their love of dance into a career.

ORGANIZATIONS

American Guild of Musical Artists
1430 Broadway, 14th Floor
New York, NY 10018
(212) 265-3687

Website: http://www.musicalartists.org
This labor union for opera performers, dancers, and concert musicians provides information to members on upcoming auditions.

Dance/USA
1029 Vermont Avenue NW, Suite 400
Washington, DC 20005
(202) 833-1717
Website: https://www.danceusa.org
This is a professional support group for people working in professional dance, including artists, administrators, and organizations.

VIDEOS

"Pop Sugar Dance Workouts"
http://www.popsugar.com/latest/Dance-workouts
These dance routines and workouts will help keep you fit.

APPS

DanceLab (George Lee)
DanceLab provides dance tutorials and news about the field of professional dance.

WEBSITES

Because of the changing nature of internet links, Rosen Publishing has developed an online list of websites related to the subject of this book. This site is updated regularly. Please use this link to access this list:

http://www.rosenlinks.com/CCWC/art

CHAPTER 2

MAKEUP ARTIST

Are you fascinated by the transforming power of makeup? Do you flip through magazines and scour online videos to learn the latest techniques for applying eye shadow and foundation? When you watch television shows or movies, are you focused on how an actor is made to look older or how a beautiful woman became a hideous monster on screen? If so, you may be a makeup artist in the making.

Makeup artists play a fundamental role in how characters are created—and how convincing they are—be it in the theater, on the screen, or in a photo spread.

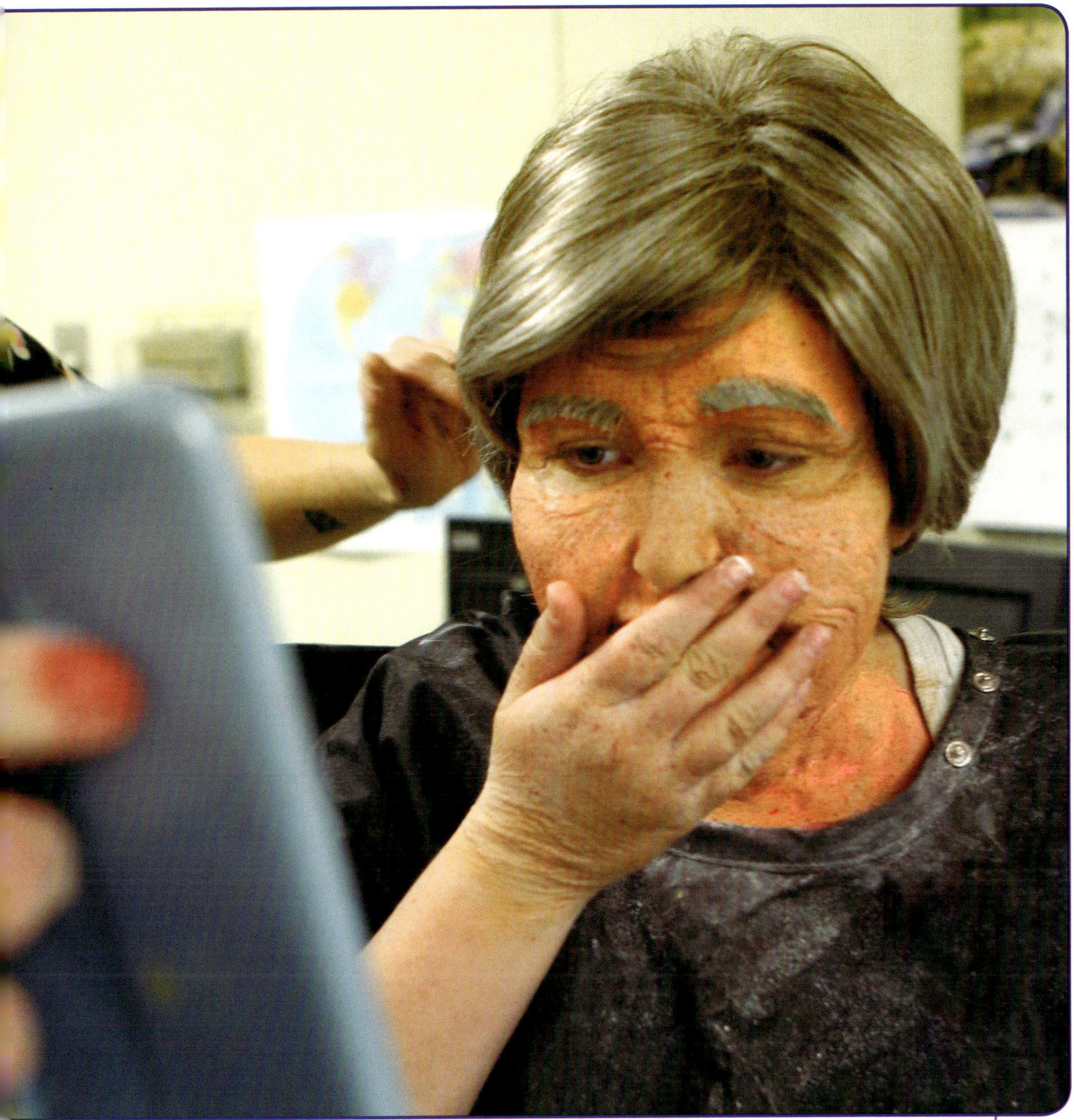

This photo shows an elementary school student seeing herself for the first time after she was made up to look like a seventy-year-old woman.

Makeup enables a person's body or face to change radically, if the person who applies it knows what he or she is doing.

A makeup artist:

- Learns various makeup techniques, including working with prosthetics
- Works with models, with actors, and in salons for the general public
- Keeps on top of emerging trends and techniques within the cosmetic industry
- Is knowledgeable about healthy skin care and the importance of hygiene relating to makeup and tools such as brushes

Makeup artists work on video, film, television, theater, and photo shoots, working with models, actors, musicians—people of all ages and walks of life. Makeup artists often use more than your typical makeup selection. If a film actor has to be transformed into an alien or monster, makeup artists use foam or other materials to create that effect.

Succeeding as a makeup artist requires a broad range of skills, but many specialize in particular techniques for altering or enhancing a person's appearance. These can include special effects, prosthetics, theatrical makeup, or high-fashion makeup.

When makeup is done perfectly, the audience believes what they are seeing is real. Achieving this effect takes hours of work—sometimes up to eight hours!

FROM PREMED TO *AMERICA'S NEXT TOP MODEL*

Jay Manuel was born in Canada in 1972 and become one of the most recognizable makeup professionals when he earned a spot on Tyra Banks's megasuccessful television reality series, *America's Next Top Model.* As creative director, Manuel was responsible for determining the look for photo shoots for the show. These challenging shoots ranged from your standard beauty photo to dramatic looks, including making up the models to look like anything from birds to marble statues or dousing them in maple syrup. According to the editors at tv.com, Manuel originally wanted to be a doctor and was studying premed at college when he decided to drop out and pursue a career as a makeup artist. He quickly landed high-fashion clients, including Tyra Banks—and the rest is fashion history.

A makeup artist works closely with a director to determine the desired outcome and figure out how to achieve it. Many makeup artists have studios, but often they will work on the set of a film, television, or photo shoot.

The most important equipment for a makeup artist is makeup and the tools used to apply it. Many makeup artists work with established cosmetic brands to develop the products they use, while other artists create their own line of cosmetics. Keeping tools such as makeup brushes clean and free from bacteria is another responsibility of the makeup artist.

PREPARING YOURSELF

To prepare yourself for a career as a makeup artist, it is important to develop an impressive portfolio of photos of your work. To build this, find work wherever you can: a friend's sweet sixteen party or other special occasion, local theater productions, ballet recitals—wherever you can show off your ability to create a desired effect with cosmetics. Seek work,

Makeup artist Veronica Ortiz turns a participant at Florida's SuperCon into a believable-looking zombie using a special technique to make the woman's skin look torn.

paid or otherwise, at a salon or cosmetic store where you can get experience and on-the-job training. Look for professional development through working in your school's theater or music program. Local beauty schools or salons may also offer tutorials and courses to help you learn and refine techniques in the art of makeup application. Develop a website to advertise your work, and over time as you build up your résumé and portfolio, you can apply to production companies or photo studios. It's a competitive field, so determination and confidence is definitely needed.

FUTURE PROSPECTS

Many makeup artists are satisfied to make life-long careers of their passion, rising up the ranks and eventually becoming creative directors for cosmetic companies. Others eventually hang up their brushes for different types of work. Job prospects for makeup artists include cosmetology—moving beyond makeup to provide things like hairstyling or manicures—which

Professional makeup artists remain on set during photo shoots or filming to do any touching up of makeup that's needed throughout the day.

requires certification, but not a college degree. Some makeup artists pursue careers as skin-care specialists, while others move away from cosmetic application and into full-time cosmetic development.

According to the Bureau of Labor Statics, jobs in the beauty business—including hairstyling, makeup artistry, and cosmetology—are expected to grow 10 percent between 2014 and 2024, and most job opportunities are found in major cities.

FOR MORE INFORMATION

BOOKS

Brown, Bobbi. *The Bobbi Brown Makeup Manual*. New York, NY: Grand Central Life & Style, 2011.

This book offers tips from makeup artist Bobbi Brown. It includes information on skin-care basics.

Eldridge, Lisa. *Face Paint: The Story of Makeup*. New York, NY: Harry N. Abrams, 2015.

A history of makeup as an art form, this book takes readers from Egyptian times to the present day.

Reyna, G. M. *How to Be a Professional Makeup Artist: A Comprehensive Guide for Beginners*. CreateSpace Independent Publishing Platform, 2013.

This career guide offers a close-up look at what it takes to become a professional makeup artist.

ORGANIZATIONS

Hair and Makeup Artist Network
121 W. Lexington Drive
Suite 332
Glendale, CA 91203
(323) 913 9375
Website: http://www.hmartistsnetwork.com

This is a nationwide organization for freelance hair and makeup professionals.

Professional Beauty Association
15825 N. 71st Street, #100
Scottsdale, AZ 85254
(800) 468-2274
Website: https://probeauty.org
The Professional Beauty Association (PBA) is the largest organization of salon professionals and provides its members with webinars and other educational opportunities, as well as providing charitable outreach to several worthy causes.

VIDEOS

"Real Techniques"
https://realtechniques.com/videos
Makeup pros Samantha and Nicola Chapman share their techniques in this series of videos.

WEBSITES

Because of the changing nature of internet links, Rosen Publishing has developed an online list of websites related to the subject of this book. This site is updated regularly. Please use this link to access this list:

http://www.rosenlinks.com/CCWC/art

CHAPTER 3

PRODUCTION ASSISTANT

Many people imagine the world of television and film production to be glamorous and exciting—and completely out of reach for the average person. The truth is, not everyone who works in these fields attended film school (including directors James Cameron and Quentin Tarantino) and many, such as Woody Allen and Walt Disney, never even attended college.

One good way to enter the film and television business is by becoming a production assistant. The production assistant is responsible for a wide range of tasks that support the process of making a television program, commercial, or feature film.

Production assistants do not operate cameras or lights or yell, "Cut!" They are an important part of the team, however, as production managers rely on assistants to make sure everything runs smoothly. Production assistants perform tasks such as bringing the "talent" (actors) to set, making sure all the necessary props are on hand, and redirecting

Production assistants must juggle a lot of different tasks and work long hours, but the job is exciting and the experience they gain invaluable.

traffic so the crew can film a key scene. No day looks exactly the same for a production assistant, and the hours can be unpredictable as well.

The work of a production assistant typically includes:

- Providing administrative support, including answering phones and photocopying scripts
- Running errands, including picking up props and talent, and ordering in food for long shoots
- Troubleshooting problems on set, such as keeping everyone quiet during filming and directing extras—actors who appear in the background but don't speak—through the set
- Redirecting traffic and picking up and dropping off actors from their homes or hotels

This demanding role can require twelve to sixteen hours of work each day, and a production assistant is often the first to arrive on set and the last to leave. However, the work is never dull. There is so much to do and the pace is so intense that you are never stuck at a desk watching the clock. Also, when shooting is done, production assistants can take a little time off before starting their next job.

Some production assistants work in house for production companies, but for the most part this is a freelance position, meaning you work for yourself and various companies contact you when there is a job available. Because of the freelance nature of this career, it is important for a production

"I NEVER KNEW WORK COULD BE SO FUN!"

Lisa DeFalco is a freelance production manager living in Hoboken, New Jersey, just across the Hudson River from Manhattan. Living a stone's throw from New York City, a hotbed of television production, has given DeFalco lots of interesting work experience since she arrived twenty years ago and began working as a production assistant. "I actually did study film, but what really launched my career was hitting the ground running as a production assistant. I called every company I could find and soon starting working on television commercials and TV movies."

DeFalco's work over the years has included nationally televised commercials, show openers, and a documentary about the making of the 2015 Super Bowl halftime show featuring Katy Perry. These days she hires production assistants herself. "If you are hardworking, if you are reliable, and if you demonstrate that you really want this work and take it seriously, I will give you a chance."

It's a production assistant's job to make sure that no one is on set except those involved in filming and that no outside noise disturbs the production.

assistant to have many contacts in the industry.

PREPARING YOURSELF

This entry-level position does not come with many educational requirements, although some production assistants have attended film school. The job mostly requires a candidate to be hardworking and passionate about his or her work. Any classes you can take in project or time management will help you juggle the many tasks for which you will be responsible. Getting involved in theater or film production at your high school or in your local community is a huge plus. You will not only gain experience but also learn to work with a wide range of personalities—a must for any successful production assistant.

The most important thing someone who wants to work as a

Production assistants have to be willing to take on any job, including transporting actors to and from the set and picking up coffee for those involved in the project.

production assistant can do is contact as many production companies or television stations as possible and demonstrate that you have what it takes to do the job well. You must convince the person doing the hiring that you have a good work ethic and a "can-do" attitude. You must be willing to take orders and follow instructions, and you must be flexible with your schedule and the types of tasks you will take on, as the demands of the job can be unpredictable. Be organized and polite, and be able to anticipate problems before they arise.

FUTURE PROSPECTS

Once you have developed a decent résumé of jobs and good relationships with various contacts through your work as a production assistant, you can use this experience to move yourself further up the film and television ladder. The next job will likely be that of production coordinator, a position that supervises production assistants, but if you want to pursue camera or lighting work, you can pursue that as well. In addition, a good production assistant can hope to participate in the Directors Guild of America training program, if recommended by the production manager.

As production assistant jobs are typically short-term, according to the Bureau of Labor Statistics, the best work can be found working on ongoing projects like television series.

FOR MORE INFORMATION

BOOKS

Ascher, Stephen, and Edward Pincus. *The Filmmaker's Handbook: A Comprehensive Guide for the Digital Age*. New York, NY: Plume, 2012.

This handbook for moviemakers includes how to find funding for your projects.

Bill, Tony. *Movie Speak: How to Talk Like You Belong on a Film Set*. New York, NY: Workman Publishing Company, 2009.

This book is full of insights into life on a film set and includes an explanation of the slang terms used on set.

Clark, Caleb. *The Production Assistant's Pocket Handbook*. Lulu.com Publishers, 2011.

Clark shares his personal experience working as a production assistant.

ORGANIZATIONS

Alliance for Women in Media
1250 24th Street NW, Suite 300
Washington, DC 20037
Website: http://www.allwomeninmedia.org

The Alliance for Women in Media is a nonprofit, professional organization for women who work in media.

DGA Assistant Director Training Program
1697 Broadway
New York, NY 10019
(212) 397-0930
Website: http://www.dgatrainingprogram.org
This organization offers opportunities for anyone wanting to become an assistant director in film, television, or commercial production.

Directors Guild of America
7920 Sunset Boulevard
Los Angeles, CA 90046
(310) 289-2000
Website: http://www.dga.org
The Directors Guild of America was established to protect the creative and economic rights of its members.

VIDEOS

"Production Assistant Tips and Tricks with Channing Duke"
https://www.youtube.com/watch?v=Ka7ZjI75pfk

This video gives a real-world glimpse into the life of a production assistant and advice on how to break into the field.

APPS

Crew Time Card (Joe Kocsis)

This app for entertainment industry crew workers helps keep track of when they are due on set, how many hours they have worked, and other items related to the work of production assistants.

GoldenLight (Videomaker)

GoldenLight tells you when the sun rises and sets on any day at any place on Earth, which is helpful information for a film production company to have.

WEBSITES

Because of the changing nature of internet links, Rosen Publishing has developed an online list of websites related to the subject of this book. This site is updated regularly. Please use this link to access this list:

http://www.rosenlinks.com/CCWC/art

CHAPTER 4

GAME ARTIST

Do you carry a sketchpad wherever you go, drawing realistic images or fantastical creatures you've dreamed up in your mind? Are you able to draw from life and create characters with recognizable facial expressions? Can you communicate an understanding of anatomy and architecture?

Along with all that, are you fascinated by video games and drawn to the strange worlds and characters they contain? Do you love figuring out the best strategies for how to play a game? If the idea of combining your passion for art with your love of

If you want to be a game artist, carry a sketchbook so you can add to your imaginary worlds full of people, weapons, and landscapes wherever you go.

"ALWAYS BE IN BETA STAGE, ALWAYS IMPROVING AND EXPANDING"

Anthony Handy is a game artist with a game development company in North Carolina. Handy's skills and drive earned him his break, even though he lacked a college degree. Handy believes that art skills are key but not enough and that who you are as a person plays a big role in your success. "Being honest, being kind and caring, knowing when to take risks, and always being hungry is important," he says. "This industry is very small and everyone knows everyone, so impressions do matter." He also says you have to be passionate about what you do, and be willing to leave your comfort zone. "Taking risks is something I did to really jump start my journey," he says. "It's because I left my hometown by myself and traveled to a brand new state and started meeting people, that's what boosted me to this level. Knowing when to really go for what you want despite the odds can definitely prove beneficial. And always be hungry, never satisfied. Always growing and expanding. Never grow complacent, never stop working hard and doing what you love, never stop learning."

gaming sounds too good to be true, working as a game artist may be the ideal job for you.

Game artists are creative, but they are also able to follow specifications (specs) and storyboards for the games they will work on. Storyboards are a set of drawings that show each scene of a video game. Artists typically work in teams, so being able to work well with other people, take direction, and communicate feedback effectively are key.

There are different types of game artists, each using various techniques in his or her work. Some of these artists include:

- Concept artist: A concept artist usually works with traditional tools, such as pen and paper, rather than computer programs. The role of a concept artist is to provide a sketch of general concepts and ideas, including how characters will look, what the setting will be, and what kinds of scenery and costumes characters will wear.
- 3D modeler: A 3D modeler uses special software to create three-dimensional images that create a game's characters, buildings, environment, setting, objects, vehicles, and furniture. Modeling is done using a variety of computer programs, such as Maya, 3DS Max, Pixar's RenderMan, POV-Ray, among others.

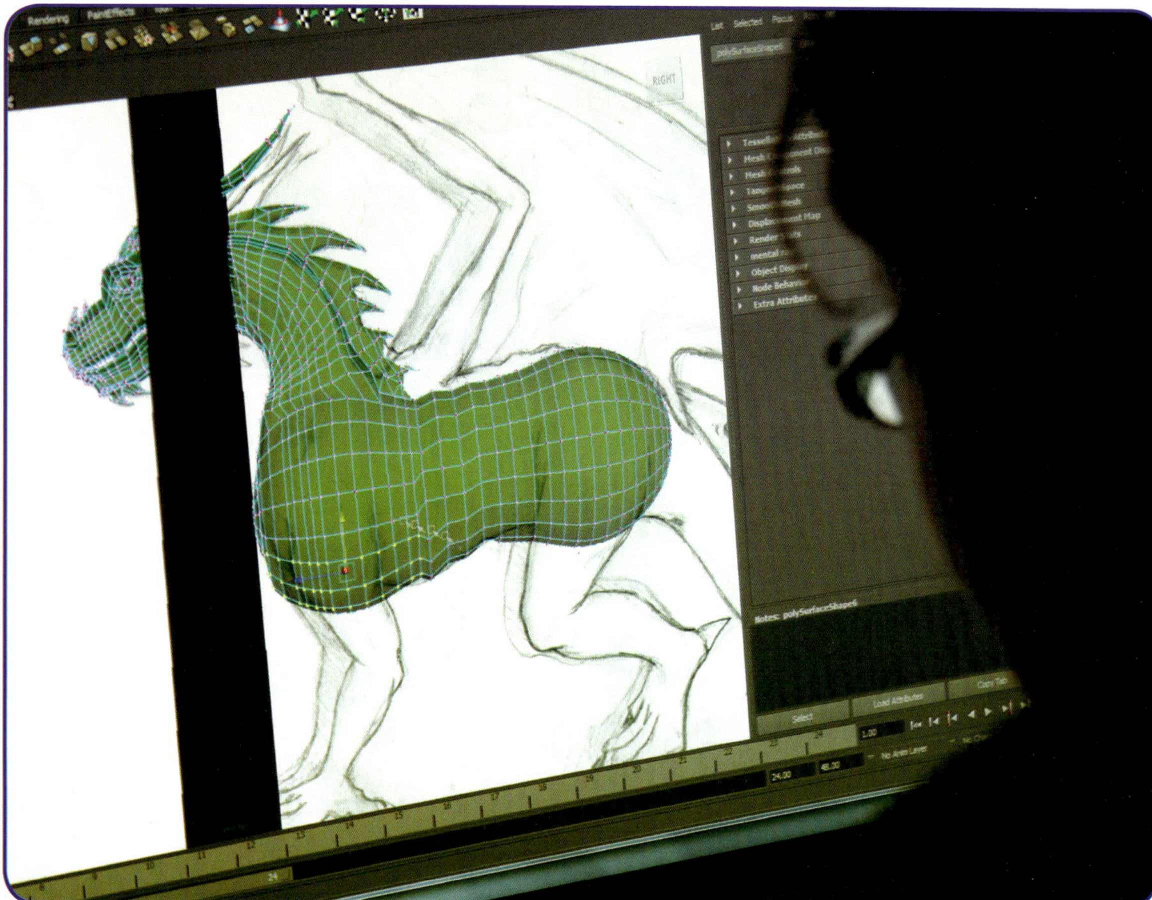

A 3D modeler is a game artist trained in using special software to make a two-dimensional drawing appear as a three-dimensional object.

- 2D/texture artist: 2D/texture artists create the setting for the game, such as a cave or a castle, as well as the objects in the game. The job of a 2D/texture artist requires considerable knowledge of lighting, perspective, materials, and visual effects.

Artists usually work under a lead artist, and they have to follow game specifications when working on their individual contributions to a game. Some artists specialize in particular aspects, such as human forms, vehicles, or environments such as caves or towns.

PREPARING YOURSELF

Some game artists hold degrees from art schools, but that is not an absolute requirement. Taking any art classes—painting, drawing, sculpture—that your high school provides will give you experience in different mediums. The job also requires technical skills, so taking any computer classes—particularly relating to graphic design or modeling—will also give you an important foundation.

On his website cybergooch.com, Eric Gooch, a gaming artist with more than fifteen years of experience in the field, states that your portfolio is more important than any degree you could earn. Collecting all of your best artwork into a physical or online portfolio and getting it into the hands of lead game developers at game development companies is the best way to land an internship, which could lead to a full-time job.

Drawing skills are a must, as is the ability to follow specs and some knowledge of the technical side of the job. Knowing how to use the required software packages and how to make the game not only look good but work on different devices and platforms is vital. Basic understanding of mathematical concepts involved in 3D graphics is also important.

Your portfolio will be your biggest asset, so it's important that it showcase your best work. Keeping informed of trends in the industry and knowing how to use the latest software, techniques, and games will also help you stand out when seeking work.

FUTURE PROSPECTS

Becoming a lead or senior artist or designing one's own game is the

A lot of planning is needed before the drawing and modeling of a video game can begin in order to make sure that all involved know how the game should look and how it should be played.

ambition of many game artists, but others leave the gaming world entirely and instead apply their skills to movies or television. Teaching drawing or the technical tools needed to be a game artist is also a possibility if the school or institution does not require its instructors to have a college degree According to the Bureau of Labor Statistics, jobs in the field of multimedia arts—including game artists—are expected to grow 6 percent between 2014 and 2024.

FOR MORE INFORMATION

BOOKS

Ceceri, Kathy. *Video Games: Design and Code Your Own Adventure*. White River Junction, VT: Nomad Press, 2015.

This study of why games are so compelling includes the history of games from ancient times to the present.

Kennedy, Sam R. *How to Become a Video Game Artist: The Insider's Guide to Landing a Job in the Gaming World*. New York, NY: Watson-Guptill, 2013.

Kennedy offers an insider's tips for having a successful career in video game art.

Solarski, Chris. *Drawing Basics and Video Game Art: Classic to Cutting-Edge Art Techniques for Winning Video Game Design*. New York, NY: Watson-Guptill, 2012.

The author provides detailed explanations of game art techniques and their importance.

ORGANIZATIONS

Graphic Artist Guild
31 West 34th Street, 8th Floor
New York, NY 10001
(212) 791-3400

Website: https://www.graphicartistsguild.org
This advocacy group focuses on raising industry standards for animators, cartoonists, designers, illustrators, and digital artists.

International Game Developers Association (IGA)
19 Mantua Road
Mt. Royal, NJ 08061
Website: http://www.igda.org
The IGA is a collection of organizations supporting professional communication design, including graphic design, visual communication, and journalism.

Society of Illustrators, Artists, and Designers (SIAD)
207 Regent Street, 3rd Floor
London W1B 3HH
England
Website: http://www.siad.org
According to its website, SIAD is a not-for-profit international professional organization that promotes "excellence in the art and technique of all visual media."

VIDEOS

"How to Sketch Game Assets"
https://www.youtube.com/watch?v=lMPV867JCgk
This video provides a tutorial in creating game assets.

APPS

iDesign app (TouchAware Limited)
This app allows you to create high-quality 2D illustrations and technical drawings.

WEBSITES

Because of the changing nature of internet links, Rosen Publishing has developed an online list of websites related to the subject of this book. This site is updated regularly. Please use this link to access this list:

http://www.rosenlinks.com/CCWC/art

CHAPTER 5

TATTOO ARTIST

Although some people still have mixed feelings about tattoos, it's hard to deny their popularity. Whereas generations ago, tattoos were often associated with rebels and sailors, today music performers, movie stars, soccer players—and many nonfamous people—are sporting ink on their bodies.

A tattoo artist:

- Puts permanent markings (drawings and/or words) on skin using ink and a specialized needle
- Consults closely with a client to design his or her desired tattoo
- Strictly follows all health codes and keeps shop equipment in sterile condition
- Stays on top of trends in tattooing and other styles of art

Drawing a tattoo on paper is an important skill, but tattoo artists also need to know how to handle the needle carefully and follow all the rules of hygiene.

An accomplished tattoo artist spends a lot of time sketching and perfecting his own unique style in order to deliver his best work to his clients.

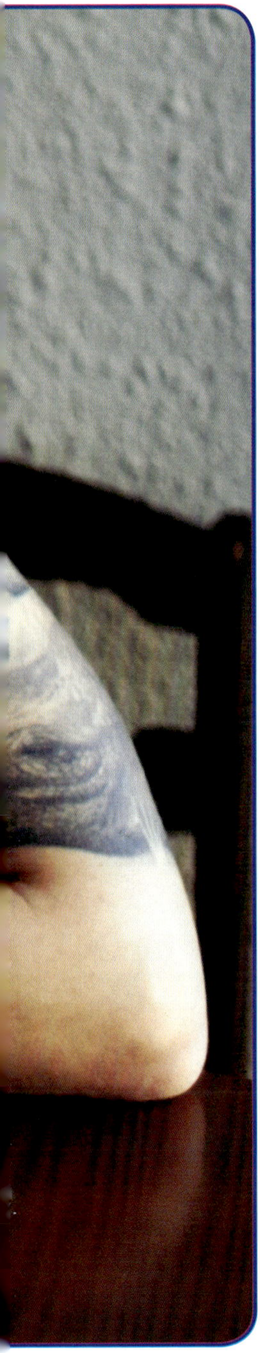

- Helps a client understand how to care for his or her tattoo
- Maintains an up-to-date license as a tattoo artist.

According to journalist Chris Weller, writing in the *Atlantic*, tattoos are more popular than ever: "In 1960, there were approximately 500 professional tattoo artists operating in the United States. By 1995, that number had risen to over 10,000. Nearly 20 years later, demand continues to surge, and by the latest estimates, roughly 20 percent of Americans have a tattoo. What's more, 40 percent of the people in that group are Millennials, which some academics argue isn't a coincidence."

It would seem from these statistics that there is room for more tattoo artists to enter the profession. And if you are a skilled artist with an interest in body art, perhaps it's your calling.

Artistic skills are a must, but there's more to succeeding as a tattoo artist than knowing how to draw. Many tattoo artists spend hours consulting with a client to design a tattoo and help that client understand where it will look best on his or her body. To prepare to apply a single tattoo, the artist must do about an hour of preparation work, depending on the size and complexity of

TOUGH TRAINING LEADS TO A SUCCESSFUL CAREER

In 2015, reporter Thomas Howells of the *Guardian* talked to British tattoo artist Phil Kyle about his start in the business. Kyle explained that after three years of trying to convince the owner of a local tattoo shop to give him an internship, he was finally given his chance at the age of twenty-one. Kyle described a "very hardcore" internship, which focused more on studio hygiene than on inking. He says those years taught him to be disciplined and safe and also showed those at the studio where he was training that he was committed to his art. "It'd be a year before interns could even touch one of those machines, aside from cleaning it," he said. "It shows how motivated you are if you stick it out." When he finally got his shot, he wasn't too nervous. "The first guy I did was covered in homemade tattoos," he said. "So anything I did couldn't be worse than that!"

the design. An artist will typically sketch the design by hand and then make a stencil or just use a pen to draw the design directly on the client's skin.

Hygiene is very important because any time you are using needles and breaking the surface of the skin there is a chance for serious infection. Properly preparing tools and keeping the studio clean—hospital-level sanitized—is crucial not only for safety but also for the reputation of a tattoo artist.

Tattoo artists must have good customer service skills. For most people, a tattoo is a permanent commitment, and a client has to trust that the artist has integrity, an eye for what will look best, and the ability to listen to the customer's needs.

PREPARING YOURSELF

To begin your journey toward working as a tattoo artist, take as many art and drawing classes as your high school offers. It's important to start building a portfolio of designs to show to tattoo studios that hire interns. You can practice by copying drawings in magazines, but also create your own designs. Just being able to draw and mimic other styles isn't enough. Tattoo artists work in a very competitive field, and it's important to build a reputation as an artist with a unique point of view.

While there's no need to get a college-level art degree, you can keep your skills sharp by taking classes or tutorials in different techniques and styles. Once you land an apprenticeship or internship, you will receive on-site training—but don't expect to be working with clients right away. It can take several years to become fully qualified as a tattoo artist.

The tattoo artist and the client must work together to make sure that the client ends up with the tattoo he truly desires.

FUTURE PROSPECTS

As with many jobs, tattoo artists often start at the bottom and work their way up, continuously learning new skills. An artist that develops a good reputation will draw more and more clients and can eventually open his or her own shop.

Despite a continuing growth in the popularity of tattoos overall, the Bureau of Labor Statistics expects a 1 percent decrease in job opportunities for tattoo artists between 2012 and 2020.

FOR MORE INFORMATION

BOOKS

Buchanan, Fip. *Drawing & Designing Tattoo Art: Creating Masterful Tattoo Art from Start to Finish*. North Fremantle, WA: Impact, 2014.

Master tattoo artist Fip Buchanan shares his expertise gained through his over thirty years of experience designing tattoo art.

Fish, Andy, and Veronica Hebard. *How to Draw Tattoo Style*. New York, NY: Chartwell Books, 2010.

This book is designed to help tattoo artists of all levels improve their artistry.

Lavell, Coen. *How to Open a Tattoo Studio Business*. CreateSpace Independent Publishing Platform, 2012.

This book outlines the steps to take to establish your own tattoo business.

ORGANIZATIONS

Alliance of Professional Tattooists (APT)
22052 W. 66th Street, Suite 225
Shawnee, KS 66226
(816) 979-1300
Website: http://www.safe-tattoos.com

According to its website, the APT's founding mission is to "address the health and safety issues facing the growing national tattoo industry."

VIDEOS

Tattoo Safety
https://www.youtube.com/watch?v=oraKFLkmVUk
This video provides information on safety concerns and regulations when getting or giving a tattoo.

APPS

Outstanding Tattoo Designs Pro (Escargot Studios, LLC)
This app has high-resolution photos and images of dramatic, detailed tattoos.

WEBSITES

Because of the changing nature of internet links, Rosen Publishing has developed an online list of websites related to the subject of this book. This site is updated regularly. Please use this link to access this list:

http://www.rosenlinks.com/CCWC/art

CHAPTER 6

PHOTOGRAPHER

Do you usually find yourself behind the lens when you are on vacation, at a party, or at a sports event? Do you carry a camera or snap photos with your smartphone wherever you go? If so, you might be interested in becoming a professional photographer, an artist whose task it is to capture amazing moments on camera.

There's more to the job than taking photos, however. A photographer must also:

- Promote himself or herself (especially if he or she

No matter what type of photograph you prefer to take, practicing your skills and building up your portfolio will help lead you toward success.

"I FOCUSED ON GETTING BETTER EACH DAY BY SHOOTING SOMETHING NEW"

Andy Kuno, the official photographer of the San Francisco Giants baseball team, believes that his skill as a photographer is based on trial and error and learning from his mistakes. Although he wanted to focus on sports photography, he stresses the importance of broadening your scope. "I just wanted to shoot games, but eventually I learned how to light subjects, shoot portraitures, and anticipate moments with a nice background. I bring all these elements to all my work now." To get started, Kuno advises landing an internship—but says your work can also get you to where you want to be. "Nowadays, it's all about internships. But if you have a wealth of experience and your work reflects that, that'll put you in a good position."

works as a freelancer) and establish good relationships with clients
- Attend events such as weddings, graduations, and sporting events, although a photographer may work only in a studio setting

- Understand natural and artificial lighting and how it affects the quality of the photograph
- Edit photographs to enhance them, using programs such as Photoshop

Photography is becoming more and more accessible to people in recent years thanks to smartphone technology, digital cameras, photo-filter apps, photo-sharing and social networking sites, and photo-editing software. Gone are the days when you had to have bulky, expensive equipment, endless rolls of film, and the time to spend hours in the darkroom in order to achieve the desired result.

The tools available today mean that most people can take a decent photograph. To become a professional, however, you need to have a unique perspective or style, and a deep understanding of how to work with light. Along with those skills, you need a good eye for composition (the position of various elements in a photo), and a unique ability to anticipate a photo-worthy moment.

If you'd like to start making money from your photos, you should first think about exactly how you will do that. Will you have a studio of your own or work on site, such as a wedding or event photographer? Will you sell prints or charge an hourly fee for photo shoots? Consider what you want to photograph and what type of specialty you might like to pursue.

Despite the high quality and ease of use of smartphone cameras, many people still hire a professional photographer for special events such as weddings.

There are many types of professional photographers, including:

- Fine art photographer
- Wedding photographer
- School portrait photographer
- Commercial or product photographer
- Baby/family photographer
- Pet photographer
- Event photographer
- Photojournalist

A photographer's work does not end when a photo shoot is over. There are still photos to edit and prints to prepare. Of course, a lot of hours will be spent speaking with clients, driving to shoot various events, and sending prints out to clients.

As is the case with many careers in the arts, professional photographers work in a competitive field. Some are in-house staff members for magazines, studios, or newspapers, and many are freelancers, seeking out job after job and building their own businesses. The ability to network and maintain a positive reputation are crucial. In addition, photographers are expected to own or rent their equipment and transportation.

A photographer should be able to form a trusting relationship with a client, be it a bride, a new parent, or a top model. Your personality and interpersonal communication skills will matter to your clients and impact how they connect with your lens. A friendly manner and good listening skills are a must.

PREPARING YOURSELF

To prepare for a career as a photographer, take photography classes or photo editing classes at your high school. Join the school newspaper or yearbook committee to improve your skills. Even if you don't plan to study photography in college, you should always look for opportunities to experiment with new techniques or tools, and seek a photo-worthy moment everywhere you go. Your portfolio should represent a wide range of work, but it should also

Photojournalists take pictures of newsworthy events such as the 1990 release of Nelson Mandela from prison, shown here. Mandela, who died in 2013, served as president of South Africa from 1994 to 1999.

highlight your unique creativity and point of view. You want your work to stand out from the crowd when you submit it to agencies, newspapers, magazines, studios, or individuals who may become employees or clients.

Build a website that showcases your best photos and gives visitors a sense of who you are and how you like to work. Ask your high school counselor to help you find out about any internships in the field of photography, any contests you can enter, or freelance opportunities that might match your skills. With his or her guidance, you can determine whether there is any additional training (individual classes at a community college, for example) you can get to jump-start your career.

FUTURE PROSPECTS

According to the Bureau of Labor Statistics, job growth for photographers between 2014 and 2024 is expected to be somewhat low, at 3 percent. Of course, some photographers go on to have extremely successful careers, publishing books or calendars of their work. Anne Geddes is widely known for her baby photographs, while Jill Greenberg is famous for her animal portraits. Many photographers go on to become photo editors or creative directors at magazines or advertising or modeling agencies.

FOR MORE INFORMATION

BOOKS

DK Publishing. *Digital Photography Complete Course*. London, England: Dorling Kindersley, 2015.

This independent photography course teaches you the ins and outs of digital photography.

Fulford, Jason. *The Photographer's Playbook: 307 Assignments and Ideas*. New York, NY: Aperture, 2014.

This is a collection of photography assignments and stories from some of the most successful and talented photographers in the world.

Northrup, Tony. *Tony Northrup's DSLR Book: How to Create Stunning Digital Photography*. Waterford, CT: Mason Press, 2012.

This hands-on, independent photography class provides more than twelve hours of online training videos.

ORGANIZATIONS

American Photographic Artists (APA)
5042 Wilshire Boulevard, #321
Los Angeles, CA 90036

Website: http://apanational.org
This organization provides members with the information and support needed to become a successful professional photographer.

American Society of Media Professionals (ASMP)
PO Box 337
Whiting, NJ 08759
Website: http://asmp.org
ASMP provides business publications for professional photographers and promotes the rights of its nearly seven thousand members.

Professional Photographers of America (PPA)
229 Peachtree Street NE, Suite 2200
Atlanta, GA 30303
(404) 522-8600
Website: http://www.ppa.com
PPA is the largest not-for-profit association dedicated to professional photographers.

VIDEOS

"7 DIY Photography Tips Using Household Objects"

https://www.youtube.com/watch?v=IH0wVcpDCok
This video contains interesting ideas for creating great photos and effects without spending a lot of money.

APPS

Filterstorm Neue (Tai Shimizu)
This app has many of the features and editing control of desktop applications like Photoshop.

Snapseed (Google, Inc.)
Snapseed is a photo-editing app that covers basic photo processing techniques, including exposure and color adjustments, cropping, and straightening.

WEBSITES

Because of the changing nature of internet links, Rosen Publishing has developed an online list of websites related to the subject of this book. This site is updated regularly. Please use this link to access this list:

http://www.rosenlinks.com/CCWC/art

CHAPTER 7

MUSIC MANAGER

Does a life on the road with your favorite band or musical artist sound too good to be true? Do you love music and dream of going to an endless list of shows and festivals? If the music industry appeals to you, but you don't dream of fronting your own band, then music management might be an appealing ambition for you.

Behind the glamour, the job of a music manager is hard work. There are two types of band manager: a road manager and a personal manager. A road manager is responsible for making sure everything goes smoothly when a band or artist is on tour. For example, a road manager books the shows and organizes transportation and accommodations for the band.

The music industry is an exciting field, but behind the scenes of every great show are a lot of people working hard to make sure the event comes together in a way that satisfies fans.

A personal manager is involved with the everyday business of the band or artist, such as working together to build a strategy for success and deciding how to get the band more publicity. A personal manager is there to guide the decisions the band or artist makes, help them create their own brand or image, and ensure they know and follow their schedule of appearances and other appointments.

Music managers who are starting out often do the work as a side job until they can earn enough to make it a full-time career. A music manager gets paid a commission, which is a set percentage of the earnings of the act they represent. Most commissions are usually 15 to 20 percent of those earnings. In order to improve your income, you need to know a lot about the music industry so you can increase earnings through licensing, publishing, merchandising, and the like.

Successful music managers have excellent communication and interpersonal skills and an insider's understanding of the music business. This means more than being passionate about a particular band or singer, as you will be in charge of publicity, record label relations, publishing relations, and other aspects of the artist's career.

The main tasks of a music manager include:

- Communicating with musicians to determine goals and objectives
- Contacting promoters, venues, and record labels to schedule meetings and performances

When a band plans a tour, the road manager books the shows and arranges transportation. This 2008 photo shows the tour bus for the Jonas Brothers.

- Scheduling and attending meetings, interviews, and appearances to promote the artist
- Communicating with merchandising companies to create artist merchandise

Your relationship to the talent you represent is key to your success as a manager. If they don't trust your instincts, or if

GRAMMY

they don't respect the commitments you've made on their behalf, the business (and in many cases personal) relationship will fail. Therefore, music managers must choose their clients wisely.

PREPARING YOURSELF

Music management requires many different skills. If your high school offers business or interpersonal communication courses or courses in managing money, these will be important classes to take. There are many colleges and universities that offer programs in music management. However, if you don't choose to go that path, you can also prepare yourself through an internship at a management company. There are also many books and seminars available on the subject. Without a proven track record, getting hired by a management company can be very difficult, so any type of work experience is valuable. Of course, finding a local band to manage is a great way to prove your skills on the job.

FUTURE PROSPECTS

The Bureau of Labor Statistics expects there to be a 9 percent growth in the music management field between 2012 and

Music industry executive David Geffen speaks at a 2011 gala in Beverly Hills, California, before the Grammy award show where he was honored for his contributions to the music industry.

DAVID GEFFEN is an American business magnate, producer, film studio executive, and philanthropist. *Forbes* magazine has called him the most powerful man in Hollywood for a generation, writing that he is "peerless in his ability to merge artistic and financial instincts." Geffen has been an agent, a manager, a leader in the recording industry, a movie and Broadway producer, and the cofounder of a film studio.

He attended the University of Texas at Austin for a semester and then Brooklyn College, before again dropping out. Geffen truly started at the bottom, beginning his career in the entertainment industry working in the mail room at the William Morris Agency (WMA). Through hard work and smart networking, Geffen quickly became a talent agent with WMA. He later left and began his own record label and is now one of the most recognized names in the music business.

2022. Living in an area with an active music scene will allow for more opportunities. Music managers can work their way up in a music management company to become music executives or expand their talent list enough to form their own agency. Some music managers can go on to work for—or even own—their own record labels.

FOR MORE INFORMATION

BOOKS

Allen, Paul. *Artist Management for the Music Business*. Waltham, MA: Focal Press, 2014.

Allen offers strategies and industry insights to help prepare you for a successful music management career.

Borg, Bobby. *Music Marketing for the DIY Musician: Creating and Executing a Plan of Attack on a Low Budget*. Milwaukee, WI: Hal Leonard Books, 2014.

This guide helps musical artists manage their time and money and get the attention of music industry professionals.

Passman, Donald. *All You Need to Know About the Music Business*. New York, NY: Simon and Schuster, 2015.

Passman's book is filled with information to prepare you for a career in an exciting but unpredictable field.

ORGANIZATIONS

Indie Managers Association (IMA)
554 N. Frederick Avenue #218
Gaithersburg, MD 20877
Website: http://www.indiemanagers.com

According to its website, this organization's mission is to "advance the cause of educating and promoting independent artist managers and self-managed artists."

Music Business Association
1 Eves Drive, Suite 138
Marlton, NJ 08053
(856) 596-2221
Website: http://musicbiz.org
The Music Business Association is a nonprofit membership organization that advances and promotes music commerce.

Music Managers Forum
Unit 31 Tileyard Studios
Tileyard Road
London, N7 9AH
England
Website: http://themmf.net
The MMF works to educate and represent managers based in the UK and connect its members to a professional network.

VIDEOS

Music Business Tutorials
https://www.lynda.com/Music-Business-training-tutorials/1752-0.html
Online courses with tutorials. Free trials are available.

Online Course in Music Management with the Berklee School of Music
https://online.berklee.edu/courses/artist-management
Learn the basics of the business online.

WEBSITES

Because of the changing nature of internet links, Rosen Publishing has developed an online list of websites related to the subject of this book. This site is updated regularly. Please use this link to access this list:

http://www.rosenlinks.com/CCWC/art

CHAPTER 8

MEDIA EQUIPMENT WORKER

Do you cringe whenever the quality of sound or lighting at a concert or other event is anything but perfect? Do you like working with technical equipment and identifying and solving problems? If you have a knack for electronics, a career as a media equipment worker might be a good fit.

Media equipment workers are responsible for ensuring that the sights and sounds of an event are up to standard, in order to provide the audience with a positive experience. These professionals are responsible for setting up, operating, and monitoring audio, video, and digital equipment for a broad range of events, including concerts, sports events, large corporate meetings, conventions, presentations, and news conferences. The job entails:

- Working with a lighting designer to design a plan for the event
- Doing risk assessments for safety purposes
- Deciding where to run cables for electrical equipment
- Helping to set up the lighting and/or sound equipment

The role of a media equipment worker is a vital one as she makes sure that all the technical aspects of an event are running smoothly. This photo shows a worker connecting cables to a sound mixer.

Media equipment workers are employed by many different industries and are valued for their technical expertise, strong communication skills, and attention to detail.

- Taking down the equipment after a show

This type of work can be found in many industries, including theater, film, television, and radio. Media equipment workers also provide their services to colleges and universities, convention centers, concert halls, and stadiums.

Sound technicians are required to assemble, operate, and maintain the technical equipment used to record, amplify, enhance, mix, or reproduce sound. Lighting technicians set up and operate lighting equipment. The work of a lighting technician requires a high degree of creativity to ensure the best lighting effects are achieved. In addition, these technicians are often required to carry heavy equipment.

Beyond being a perfectionist when it comes to the quality of sights and sounds at an event, a media equipment worker must have mechanical and telecommunications skills, as well as an ability to troubleshoot problems as they arise. He or she must also know how to install and repair equipment. These skills are usually acquired during a three to six month on-the-job training.

Most media equipment workers are freelancers, although some production companies do hire full-time media workers. As a freelancer, you are responsible for seeking out employment, which means having the confidence and drive to network and build your reputation. It is important to develop a track record that shows you are creative, responsible, professional, and reliable.

This photo shows a lighting technician watching a dress rehearsal of a theater production called *The Snowman* in London, England.

MISTAKES IN SOUND CAN RUIN A PERFORMANCE

Like many behind-the-scenes jobs in the arts, the role of the media equipment worker is such that, if you are doing your job well, nobody really notices—but if you make a mistake, it's obvious to everyone.

At the 2016 Grammy Awards, singer Adele's performance was tainted by a sound glitch. At the start of her song, a microphone fell on the strings of a piano that was accompanying her onstage, resulting in a loud guitar noise. The singer sounded flat throughout, struggling with a faulty earpiece, which is what singers wear to stay in tune during live performances. "That was all an issue on our behalf," Recording Academy president Neil Portnow told *Variety's* Alex Stedman, when discussing the audio issues. "[Grammys producer] Kenny [Ehrlich] asked that we make that really clear to everybody." Adele handled it well, saying only that this kind of thing happens. It also, Adele said, meant she got to treat herself herself to a fast food hamburger to soothe her nerves after the Grammys. "Maybe it was worth it," she joked in a tweet.

PREPARING YOURSELF

High school classes in electronics will give you a better understanding of the safety requirements needed to work with technical equipment. Your drama department, glee club, or sports department may provide opportunities to learn how to use sound and lighting equipment, as well as how to design light and sound programs for presentations.

A good way to prepare for a career as a media equipment manager is to become an apprentice to someone already doing the job. This person can show you the technical skills needed to bring someone's artistic vision to life. He or she can train you in the safety regulations and other considerations you need to keep in mind on the job.

FUTURE PROSPECTS

With some additional certification, lighting technicians can go on to specialize in areas such as electrical safety, inspection and testing, and pyrotechnics. Sound technicians can move on to find employment opportunities as a recording engineer, mixing engineer, audio operator, dubbing room engineer, broadcast engineer, or mastering engineer. According to the Bureau of Labor Statistics, the job market will grow 7 percent between 2012 and 2022, mostly through businesses, schools, and radio stations.

FOR MORE INFORMATION

BOOKS

Boonstra, Gregg. *Mixing Live Sound: An Application Guide for the Audio Technician*. CreateSpace Independent Publishing Platform, 2015.

This step-by-step guide explains how to mix live sound for a band or a show.

Box, Harry. *Set Lighting Technician's Handbook: Film Lighting Equipment, Practice, and Electrical Distribution*. Waltham, MA: Focal Press, 2013.

Box's book focuses on the importance of trouble-shooting, teamwork, and safety on set.

Shelley, Steven Louis. *A Practical Guide to Stage Lighting*. Waltham, MA: Focal Press, 2013.

Shelley offers information about the preparation that goes into creating a lighting strategy.

ORGANIZATIONS

Audio Engineering Society (AES)
551 Fifth Avenue, Suite 1225
New York, NY 10176
(212) 661-8528
Website: http://www.aes.org

The AES is the only professional society devoted exclusively to audio technology.

Society of Professional Audio Recording Services (SPARS)
(800) 771-7727
Website: http://www.spars.com
Members of SPARS have access to a network of the best-known and most successful professionals in the industry.

United States Institute for Theatre Technology (USITT)
315 S Crouse Avenue, Suite 200
Syracuse, NY 13210
Website: http://www.usitt.org
USITT is an association of design, production, and technology professionals in the performing arts and entertainment industry.

VIDEOS

"Rock Concert Lighting Design"
https://www.youtube.com/watch?v=ebhRj-dxnWE
This video provides creative ideas for achieving effects with lighting at a concert.

APPS

Soundboard Studio (JoeAllenPro Limited)

This app provides a sound studio for podcasters, DJs, voice presenters, and others.

WEBSITES

Because of the changing nature of internet links, Rosen Publishing has developed an online list of websites related to the subject of this book. This site is updated regularly. Please use this link to access this list:

http://www.rosenlinks.com/CCWC/art

CHAPTER 9

COSTUME DESIGNER

Is your favorite part of a film or play the clothes? Do you love costume parties and have an eye for accessorizing? If you have an appreciation for fashion and the creativity and skills to sketch designs and bring them to life, costume design could be the field for you.

Costume designers are an essential part of any performance, be it theater, television, film, or dance. It matters what performers wear because costumes help express who a character is. Costumes help an audience understand the year or period of a piece, whether it's the distant past or the faraway future.

Costume designers have to have both creative and technical skills. They use many different tools to create their costumes and are always prepared with what they need to make adjustments or repairs to their creations.

Julie Lynch, an Australian costume designer, during a fitting with an actor at the Sydney Opera House in Sydney, Australia. Lynch works in theater, television, opera, and dance.

Costumes need to appear authentic to the personality, time, place, and situation of a production. A designer must be a fashion professional and be able to design, sew, research, and buy clothing for characters. It also entails selecting accessories or props to help create the sense of a character.

A costume designer must:

- Carefully review a script or storyline of a performance to understand the characters and the period
- Draft a "costume plot," which is a series of sketches, photographs, and other images to convey what a character will wear
- Once the costume plot is approved, the designer will begin sewing, purchasing items, and arranging fittings for costumes
- When a show's run is over, the costume designer is responsible for returning any borrowed costumes or accessories

The costume designer might do all of the work in smaller productions or work with and oversee a team of tailors for larger performances.

Costume design is hard work and often requires working long hours. Some costumes designers work eighteen-hour days for weeks on end to keep on schedule and achieve the desired look.

Costume designers have to maintain a budget and be responsible for returning borrowed costumes or accessories after a production is finished. Good time management skills are key, as are interpersonal skills. Costume designers have to be able to interpret

A costumer is shown looking for a particular item in the costume warehouse that stores the clothes for a Shakespeare festival in Ontario, Canada.

"DO NOT WAIT TO BE TAUGHT"

Ellen McCartney is head of costume design at the California Institute for the Arts. On a site called TheArtCareerProject.com, she gives this advice to future costume designers: "Do not wait to be taught. Theatre is one of the most welcoming of all the art communities. If you are curious, do not be shy about approaching a local theatre to volunteer. Being a costume designer for live performance or film is a lifestyle and sometimes a fast paced one. Experience is the best way to know if you like the lifestyle or not. In terms of preparing skills, start taking drawing and painting lessons *early*. Draw from life and draw every day. Costume designers need to be keenly observant of the world around them, and drawing is a way to observe, record and develop a skill."

and follow directions and communicate with everyone involved in the production when creating a design.

Costume designers are often freelancers and can be based in a studio or work from home. However, designers are often required to attend meetings at theaters or television or film production companies and must be available for fittings or repairs on set throughout the run of the production.

PREPARING YOURSELF

The best way to prepare yourself for a career as a costume designer is to live and breathe fashion and hone your sketching and sewing skills. If your high school offers drawing or sewing classes, it is a good idea to immerse yourself in these activities as much as you can to develop your skills. Get involved in school productions to gain experience in the field. Taking classes in literature and film can help you understand the creation of a character and visualize a scene.

Getting work at a local theater is a good way to develop your expertise and build a portfolio. Costume design is a highly competitive field, so you have to have a lot of drive and confidence to be successful. Working with a seamstresses, taking drawing classes, and studying the history of costume design will also help you prepare for a costume design career.

FUTURE PROSPECTS

Many costume designers begin as assistants and work their way up to senior level designers, managing teams for large performances. Costume designers can also become fashion designers or work with creative departments at fashion magazines. The Bureau of Labor Statistics does not give specific prospects for costume designers, but overall the job market for clothing designers is projected to decrease by 3 percent between 2012 and 2022.

FOR MORE INFORMATION

BOOKS

Kyoto Costume Institute. *Fashion: A History from the 18th to the 20th Century*. Los Angeles, CA: Taschen, 2015.

The Kyoto Costume Institute is dedicated to understanding clothes from a sociological, historical, and artistic perspective.

Landis, Deborah Nadoolman. *Film Craft: Costume Design*. Waltham, MA: Focal Press, 2012.

Sixteen of the world's leading costume designers share their experience and knowledge with the reader.

Walter Foster Creative Team. *How to Draw & Paint Fashion & Costume Design: Artistic Inspiration and Instruction from the Vintage Walter Foster Archives*. Irvine, CA: Walter Foster Publishing, 2012.

This collection of fashion sketches provides inspiration for creating fashion using a variety of media.

ORGANIZATIONS

Costume Designer's Guild
11969 Ventura Boulevard, 1st Floor
Studio City, CA 91604

(818) 752-2400
Website: http://costumedesignersguild.com
This guild represents costume designers working in motion pictures, television, and commercials.

Costume Society
150 Aldersgate Street
London, EC1A 4AB
England
Website: http://www.costumesociety.org.uk
This organization promotes the study and preservation of historic and contemporary dress.

National Costumers Association
Website: http://www.costumers.org
The National Costumers Association brings together a small group of costumers dedicated to promoting the costume industry.

VIDEO

"The Costume Designer (Career Guides)"

http://www.youtube.com/watch?v=UOWOwzGw6C0

This is a career guide to working in costume design.

APP

Sewing Kit (Vesta Software, LLC)
This app offers tools and notes for costumers, designers, and sewing pros.

WEBSITES

Because of the changing nature of internet links, Rosen Publishing has developed an online list of websites related to the subject of this book. This site is updated regularly. Please use this link to access this list:

http://www.rosenlinks.com/CCWC/art

CHAPTER 10

ACTOR

Many people have dreamed of lighting up the silver screen and delivering an Oscar speech. It's hard not to wonder what it would be like to live the glamorous Hollywood life, star on everyone's favorite television show, or shine on Broadway. If you long for the spotlight, enjoy transforming into character, and have a wealth of drive and ambition, the actor's life might be for you.

To work as an actor, one has to:

- Read scripts and continuously audition for parts
- Fully understand the motivations behind a character's actions and feelings and be able to convey them believably for an audience
- Memorize lines in a script and deliver them seamlessly

The cast of the play *Something Rotten* is shown here performing at the St. James Theatre in New York City on the four hundredth anniversary of William Shakespeare's death.

- Attend promotional events and give interviews in the media to support projects

Acting is a very competitive field, and actors must always be looking for their next gig. Some actors are lucky enough to land a role on a television series that runs for a decade, but most actors work project by project and must be prepared for spells where they are not being paid to act. A lot of actors have side jobs for that purpose, such as working with a temporary work placement agency or as a waiter.

Actors often work with agents who help them find jobs. Getting an agent doesn't guarantee you work, but it can make it easier to get auditions. Being an actor involves a lot of auditioning, for anything from a film role to voice-over on the radio. Because the work can vary so much, it is important to have range as an actor. Location is also a factor. To get bigger jobs, it's best to live near a city where the opportunities will be more readily available rather than somewhere more remote.

Being an actor takes commitment, resilience, a thick skin, and perseverance. It is a profession that comes with a lot of rejection that may not even have to do with your acting skills. Most directors are looking for a certain type to fill a role, and the decision of whom to cast is reliant on many factors other than just acting talent. There can be comments made about your body size, ethnic background, or simply the perceived connection between two actors on set.

Actors who are just starting out have to audition for roles in film, television, or the theater continually. There is a lot of rejection in the business, so it's important to believe in yourself.

These acting students are shown listening to a director in a drama class. Like most people working in the arts, actors need to practice their craft in order to have successful careers.

PREPARING YOURSELF

Being part of your school's drama or glee club is a place to develop your talent. You can study acting in college, but it's not a requirement. What is important is that you gain experience wherever you can—local theater, local television stations—and build a résumé of work that shows off your skills.

Look for work as an extra—a "background" actor in film or television who appears on screen but doesn't have a speaking role. And always be learning: enroll in classes at a local college or seek out workshops and develop skills that don't immediately have to do with acting—singing or dance lessons, for example. Build up that résumé!

FUTURE PROSPECTS

The job outlook for actors is strong, according to the Bureau of Labor Statistics, which projects the job market will grow 10 percent between 2014 and 2024.

"THE WORK HAS TO FILL YOUR HEART"

Susan Lombardi-Verticelli has acted in a variety of projects, from voice-over work to theater to infomercials, and she says being an actor has meant learning about making her own way. "The work has to fill your heart; if it doesn't it is time to move on, as I have thought about doing so many times." She also says it's possible to make a living as an actor without focusing on starring roles and national ads. "It's about all the in-betweens that make it possible. Jobs I didn't know were out there for actors: corporate role plays to help employees understand their 'role' in their organization, educational theatre; and working with students, or simulating an illness to help a doctor communicate more effectively with their patients, demos that live on forever on the internet... jobs are all around." Her advice for finding work: "Finding mentors, taking classes, and asking questions, much like other professions, help the actor create a network and hopefully create more work."

Actors can continue to perform on stage or screen for the whole of their careers, but many actors decide to branch out into other areas of production, such as writing, producing, or directing. Successful actors can also teach acting.

FOR MORE INFORMATION

BOOKS

Brown, D. W. *You Can Act!: A Complete Guide for Actors.* Studio City, CA: Michael Wiese Productions, 2009.

This guide to acting was written by the former coach of stars such as Halle Berry, Dustin Hoffman, and Robert DeNiro.

Kerr, Judy. *Acting Is Everything: An Actor's Guidebook for a Successful Career in Los Angeles.* London, England: September Publishing, 2015.

An acting coach shares her lifetime of techniques and tricks of the trade.

ORGANIZATIONS

Academy of Motion Picture Arts and Sciences (AMPAS)
8949 Wilshire Boulevard
Beverly Hills, CA 90211-1972
(310) 247-3000
Website: http://www.oscars.org

This organization of motion-picture professionals was founded to advance the art and science of motion pictures.

Alliance of Motion Pictures & Television Producers (AMPTP)
15503 Ventura Boulevard, Bldg. E
Sherman Oaks, CA 91436
(818) 995-3600
Website: http://www.amptp.org
The AMPTP is a trade association involved with labor issues within the motion picture and television industries.

VIDEOS

"Acting Lesson for Kids: Short Scene Study"
https://www.youtube.com/watch?v=7iecQ6vNEt4
These short acting lessons are for kids, teens, and young adults.

"Ten Ways to Practice Improvisation Acting Skills"
https://www.youtube.com/watch?v=SDSP8wYlMzY
This video tutorial was designed to improve an actor's improvisational skills.

APP

Scene Partner (mytheaterapps, LLC)
This app helps actors memorize their lines.

WEBSITES

Because of the changing nature of internet links, Rosen Publishing has developed an online list of websites related to the subject of this book. This site is updated regularly. Please use this link to access this list:

http://www.rosenlinks.com/CCWC/art

GLOSSARY

AMPLIFY To make a sound louder, often by means of technical equipment.

ANATOMY An area of scientific study that examines the underlying structure of plants and animals.

APPRENTICE A person who is learning a trade from a skilled professional.

AUDITIONING The process of trying out for a part in a performance.

CERTIFICATION Proof of having the correct skills or knowledge to perform a task, usually received after taking an exam.

CHOREOGRAPHY The art of arranging dance movement and sequences.

CONSULTING Communication with a customer or coworker in order to make decisions.

COSMETICS Makeup that is applied to enhance or change the appearance of a person's face.

DUBBING A process by which additional music or dialogue is added to a film or TV show.

FEEDBACK Information about how a person reacts to someone or something.

FREELANCER A person who works for himself or herself rather than for a company.

GUILD An association of people in a similar field who work for the greater good of the profession, such as deciding on minimum pay.

HYGIENE A set of behaviors designed to keep one clean and healthy.

INTERNSHIP An opportunity to gain work experience through on-the-job training. Internships are often unpaid.

MERCHANDISE Items that are put up for sale.

PORTFOLIO A collection of photos or drawings that represent an artist's body of work.

PRODUCTION The process of making a film, television show, play, or dance program.

PYROTECHNICS A display of fireworks, often used in a performance setting.

RÉSUMÉ A document that lists a person's work history and qualifications for employment.

SPECIFICATIONS A detailed description of the design and materials used to make something.

TATTOO A design created by inserting ink into the skin.

BIBLIOGRAPHY

American Association of Community Theater. "The Costume Designer's Job." Retrieved April 2, 2016. http://www.theartcareerproject.com/become-costume-designer.

Art Careers Project. Retrieved April 2, 2016. http://www.theartcareerproject.com/art-as-a-career.

Creative Skillset. "Costume Designer." Retrieved April 4, 2016. http://creativeskillset.org/job_roles/1756_costume_designer.

DeFalco, Lisa. Email interview with the author. April 10, 2016.

Doskocil, Melanie. "15 Truths About Being a Professional Dancer." The Portland Ballet. Retrieved April 1, 2016. http://theportlandballet.org/15-truths-professional-dancer.

Forbes. "The World's Billionaires." Retrieved May 16, 2016. http://www.forbes.com/profile/david-geffen.

Gooch, Eric. "Getting a Job as a Games Artist." Cyber Gooch. Retrieved April 3, 2016. http://www.cybergooch.com/tutorials/pages/gamejob/getting_a_games_art_job.htm.

Handy, Anthony. Email interview with the author. March 11, 2016.

Howells, Thomas. "How Do I Become ... a Tattoo Artist?" *Guardian*, May 19, 2015. http://www.theguardian.com/money/2015/may/19/how-become-tattoo-artist-phil-kyle.

King, Thomas. *The Operator: David Geffen Builds, Buys, and Sells the New Hollywood*. New York, NY: Broadway Books, 2001.

King, Tyler, ed. "Production Assistant." GetInMedia.com. Retrieved April 2, 2016. http://getinmedia.com/careers/production-assistant.

Kuno, Andy. Email interview with the author. April 2, 2016.

Lac, Karen. *Madonna: Biography of the World's Greatest Pop Singer*. San Francisco, CA: Hyperink, 2012.

Laryssa. "How to Get a Job as a Production Assistant." Needle Girl. Retrieved April 2, 2016. http://needlegirlhaystackworld.com/how-to-get-a-job-as-a-production-assistant.

Lomardi-Verticelli, Susan. Email interview with the author. March 15, 2016.

McRae, Alex. "I Want Your Job: Tattoo artist." *Independent*. September 20, 2007. http://www.independent.co.uk/student/career-planning/getting-job/i-want-your-job-tattoo-artist-464450.html.

nPhoto. "How to Become a Professional Photographer." *Digital Camera World*. February 2, 2015. http://www.digitalcameraworld.com/2015/02/02/become-professional-photographer.

Rudulph, Heather Wood. "Get That Life: How I Became a Celebrity Make-up Artist." Cosmopolitan.com, May 25, 2015. http://www.cosmopolitan.com/career/news/a40801/get-that-life-monika-blunder-makeup-artist.

Smith, Jacquelyn. "The 35 highest-paying jobs you can get without a bachelor's degree." *Business Insider*, October 23, 2015. http://uk.businessinsider.com/high-paying-jobs-dont-require-bachelors-degree-2015-10?r=US&IR=T).

Stedman, Alex. "Grammys: Adele, Recording Academy President Explain Audio Glitch." *Variety*, February 15, 2016. http://variety.com/2016/music/news/grammys-adele-audio-glitch-grammy-awards-2016-1201706861.

TV.com. "Jay Manuel biography." Retrieved May 16, 2016. http://www.tv.com/people/jay-manuel/trivia.

Weller, Chris. "The Identity Crisis Under the Ink." *Atlantic*. November 25, 2014 (http://www.theatlantic.com/health/archive/2014/11/the-identity-crisis-under-the-ink/382785).

INDEX

P

R

S

T

W

ABOUT THE AUTHOR

Tracy Brown Hamilton is a journalist and blogger and the author of many books for young adults. She currently lives in the Netherlands with her husband and three children.

PHOTO CREDITS

Cover, p. 1 Dragon Images/Shutterstock.com; pp. 4–5 Simone Golob/Corbis/Getty Images; pp. 8–9 Kathrin Ziegler/DigitalVision/Getty Images; pp. 10–11 irenetinta/E+/Getty Images; pp. 12–13, 44–45 Jutta Klee/The Image Bank/Getty Images; pp. 20–21 Brian Vander Brug/Los Angeles Times/Getty Images; pp. 24–25 Rhona Wise/AFP/Getty Images; pp. 26–27 Cultura RM Exclusive/Marcel Weber/Getty Images; p. 33 Comstock/Stockbyte/Getty Images; pp. 36–37 David McNew/Getty Images News; pp. 38–39 Paul Bradbury/CalaImage/Getty Images; p. 48 Christian Science Monitor/Getty Images; pp. 50–51 Klaus Vedfelt/Taxi/Getty Images; pp. 56–57 Westend61/Getty Images; pp. 58–59 PeopleImages/DigitalVision/Getty Images; p. 62 Marco Secchi/Getty Images News; pp. 66–67 Arctic-Images/Taxi/Getty Images; pp. 70–71 Jamie Grill/The Image Bank/Getty Images; pp. 72–73 Peter Turnley/Corbis Historical/Getty Images; pp. 78–79 Guy Prives/Moment/Getty Images; p. 81 Mondadori Portfolio/Getty Images; p. 82 Kevork Djansezian/Getty Images; p. 89 Mika/Corbis/Getty Images; p. 90 Hero Images/Getty Images; p. 92 Oil Scarff/Getty Images News; p. 98–99 Africa Studio/Shutterstock; pp. 100–101 Fairfax Media/Getty Images; pp. 102–103 Kelly/Mooney Photography/Corbis Documentary/Getty Images; pp. 110–111 Adela Loconte/WireImage/Getty Images; p. 112 Emmanuel Faure/The Image Bank/Getty Images; pp. 114–115 Hill Street Studios/Blend Images/Getty Images; interior pages graphic (paint brush) Wiktoria Pawlak/Shutterstock.com.

Designer: Brian Garvey; Editor: Jennifer Landau; Photo researcher: Nicole Baker